JAMES
STEVENSON

"Could Be Worse!"

GREENWILLOW BOOKS, A Division of William Morrow & Company, Inc., New York

"Could Be Worse!"

At Grandpa's house things were always the same.

Grandpa always had the same thing for breakfast. Every day he read the paper.

And he always said the same thing.

No matter what.

One day Mary Ann said, "How come Grandpa never says anything interesting?
"I guess it's because nothing interesting happens to him," said Louie.

Next morning at breakfast Grandpa said something different.
He said, "Guess what!

Last night, when I was asleep,

a large bird pulled me out of bed and took me for a long ride

and dropped me in the mountains.

I heard a noise. It was an abominable snowman with a huge snowball

which he threw at me.

I got stuck inside the snowball, which rolled down the mountain.

It finally landed on the desert and began to melt.

I walked across the desert. Suddenly

I heard footsteps coming nearer and nearer.

A moment later I got squished by a giant something-or-other.

Before I could get up, I heard a strange noise.
A great blob of marmalade was coming toward me.

It chased me across the desert until . . .

I crashed into something tall. It was sort of like an ostrich and very cross.

It gave me a big kick. I went up into some storm clouds,

almost got hit by lightning, fell out of the clouds,

and landed in an ocean. I sank down about a mile to the bottom.

I saw an enormous goldfish coming at me.

I swam away as fast as I could and hid under a cup that had air in it.

When it was safe, I crawled out. I started to walk, but my foot got stuck

in the grip of a gigantic lobster.

I didn't know what to do. But just then a big squid came along

and squirted black ink all over the lobster. I escaped and

hitched a ride on a sea turtle that was going to the top for a bit of sunshine. I was fortunate to find a piece of toast floating by and rode to shore,

where I discovered a newspaper. I quickly folded it into an airplane

and flew across the sea

and back home to bed.

Now, what do you think of that?"

Behind the Scenes

Introduction

In *"Could Be Worse!"* Grandpa dreams of all kinds of animals. Although Grandpa meets them only in his imagination, his dream is partly real. There are, in fact, so many animals around us all the time—big and little, wild and tame, crawling, walking and flying—it's surprising we don't bump into them. Or maybe we do.

Snakes Alive

Here are some snake facts you might not know:

- Snakes are not slimy.
- Worms are insects, but snakes are reptiles.
- All reptiles are cold-blooded. This means that their body temperature is the same as the air around them.
- Most snakes are harmless to people and pets

Where They Came From

One hundred million (100,000,000) years ago reptiles already roamed the earth. The largest reptiles were the dinosaurs, the smallest were the lizards. Some of these lizards changed over a long period of time.

This change is called *evolution*. Their bodies grew longer. They lost their legs. This would not have happened if these changes would not make it easier for the reptile to survive in its environment.

How They Move

Although snakes are not the fastest creatures alive—the speediest travels at only 4 mph compared to you on your bike at approximately 10 mph—the way in which they move is unique. They move with a wavelike forward motion by tightening their body muscles and then relaxing them again and again. They look as if they're traveling along on a S-shaped track. The word for this kind of movement is *serpentine*. Anything S-shaped, by the way, can be called serpentine.

Snake Senses

Sight and smell are very important to snakes. Their eyes see only moving objects, which to a snake mean either food or an enemy. The sense of smell is located on the tip of its tongue, which gathers air samples to process in its mouth. As you can imagine, this design works far better than a nose would on a crawling creature like the snake. A snake, on the other hand, has no sense of hearing. It only knows a person or animal is coming when it feels vibrations on the ground.

How They Grow

Baby snakes grow very fast. Being little in the wild is not an advantage. Later the rate of growth depends on how much food a snake can get. Stories are told of South American snakes that grow to be 35 feet long.

Since snakes keep growing as long as they live, they have to shed their old skins when they get too tight. A new skin is always forming underneath the present one. If you kept a pet snake, you could see how much your pet had grown by comparing two shed skins.

Someday you might find a snakeskin on a walk in the woods. Keep it as a souvenir of this wonderful wild creature. To make a display box for your snakeskin, line a shoe box lid with a colored fabric, tape the snakeskin to the fabric and put your display on a shelf where everyone can see it.

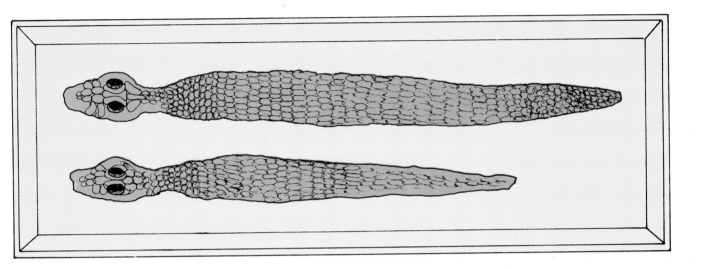

Animal Teamwork

Two animals on the same team won't be playing basketball—except maybe a giraffe and a kangaroo—but animals do sometimes work together for each other's benefit.

The shark and a small fish called a *remora,* or pilot fish, travel around together like the best of pals. The remora cleans the shark's body by eating the algae that cling to it. In return, the shark protects the remora from other fish.

Behind the Scenes

In the jungle, monkeys who live in the trees can see lions approaching. They scream an alarm that warns the zebra.

But animals do not have to get along with each other to have useful relationships. Sheepdogs, for example, could not herd sheep if they liked each other so much they'd prefer to play all day in the meadow instead.

And can you imagine rabbits and foxes, natural enemies, cooperating? Yet they share the same home. How? Not at the same time, that's how. It happens that several animals dig *burrows* to live in — rabbits, woodchucks, badgers, foxes and wolves. A burrow is a tunnel into the ground with a nest for sleeping, a pantry for food and a back door for a quick escape. A rabbit lives in a burrow called a warren. A fox lives in a burrow called a den. Often a larger animal takes over a smaller animal's burrow when it leaves. The new owner cleans the burrow, makes it larger and settles in to make it its own — for a while.

Lifestyles of the Wild and Woolly

Every animal fits into the world in a special way. Let's look at some of them.

Amphibians

Frogs, toads and salamanders live partly in the water and partly on land. Animals that live both on land and in the water are called *amphibians*. Amphibian animals have gills to breathe water when they are first born and then grow lungs when it is time to move onto the land. With lungs, animals can breathe air.

Toads live more on land than in water. You may find a toad out looking for food in a garden or in a wood. Toads and frogs look a lot alike, only a toad's skin is nubby.

Frogs like water better than land. Listen for them on a summer evening in the country if you're near a lake or a pond. Tree frogs peep. Bullfrogs croak. Toads sing. To make a noise, a frog or a toad fills its throat with air until it looks like a balloon. Then the air plays over its vocal cords and out comes sound.

Behind the Scenes

Underwater Mammals

Mammals are *warm-blooded* animals. This means that their body temperature is the same all the time because it is heated from within. *Cold-blooded* animals have a body temperature that rises and falls with the air or water around them. Humans are mammals, and dogs and cats are too. Fish are not mammals. They are cold-blooded.

You wouldn't expect to find mammals in the sea, would you? Yet the largest animal that ever lived is an underwater mammal—the blue whale. It grows to one hundred feet in length. Baby blue whales weigh over 40 tons (that's 80,000 pounds) and grow this immense by eating tiny creatures called plankton that float or drift in oceans.

A more familiar underwater mammal is the dolphin, also called a porpoise. Dolphins live in nearly every ocean and most of them stay close to land. At anywhere from 4 feet to 30 feet in length, dolphins are very friendly to people. Often they swim alongside ships.

Dolphins hear a wide variety of high and low pitched sounds. Their eyesight is also good. However, they have no sense of smell at all. What makes them special in the senses department is their natural *sonar*. Sonar means dolphins can find objects underwater by making clicking or whistling sounds. Echoes of these sounds bounce off the object. By listening to these echoes, the dolphin knows where the object is and how far away it is.

Scientists believe dolphins are among the most intelligent animals. Dolphins have long been trained to perform tricks and stunts in zoos, aquariums and amusement parks.

Recently a few trained dolphins were put up overnight at a motel swimming pool. A hurricane was about to hit their home at an aquarium and they were rushed to safety at the motel. The other guests enjoyed having them. The dolphins were entertaining throughout the night and kept everyone's mind off the storm.

Ceremonial Animals

If you remember the doves flying over the stadium at the Los Angeles Olympics, you have seen animals used in a ceremony. This means the animals stand for an idea. Something that stands for an idea is called a *symbol*. In this case, the doves became a symbol of peace, which is one of the goals of the Olympics.

Other animals stand for ideas, too—they are symbolic. Cows in India, for example, are considered holy. People do not eat cows in India for this reason.

Behind the Scenes

The eagle is an important symbol to Native American culture and many ceremonies are inspired by the eagle's power and beauty. The eagle is still the most well-known symbol of America.

In your hometown parades, the horse is often an important part of the ceremony. Next time you see a parade, look to see if the horses have special braids in their manes and tails, and if the riders are in special costumes.

Almost every state in the country has a state animal that has been chosen for its special qualities. Go to your library and look up your state animal. Why do you think it was chosen?

Now and Then

Post Office on the Hoof

When the mail arrives every day at the same time, you aren't surprised. Letters, post cards and packages fly all over the world in one or two days. Much of the work is done by machines. But long ago, mail came once in a while. Men on horseback raced across mountains and plains risking their lives to deliver it.

In 1861 it took 24 days for mail to reach California from Missouri by stagecoach. The Pony Express was started to shorten this time. It claimed to be able to deliver mail in only 10 days, and it did. But it wasn't easy.

Between St. Joseph, Missouri, and Sacramento, California, there were 190 station stops. A Pony Express rider took the mail in bags and rode from station to station. At each station, a man kept fresh horses, food and drink for the rider. Most stops were very quick — only long enough to change horses. A rider needed about 75 ponies to finish his trip. The riders earned from $100 to $150 a month and had to carry guns and knives to protect themselves from bandits. They rode in all kinds of weather, day and night. The fastest Pony Express ride carried President Lincoln's Inaugural Address to California in seven and a half days. By 1862, telegraph wires stretched from coast to coast, carrying messages across country in a few hours, so the Pony Express was no longer needed.

The Post Office today still takes pride in good service. Its motto: "Neither snow, nor rain, nor heat, nor gloom of night stays these couriers from the swift completion of their appointed rounds."

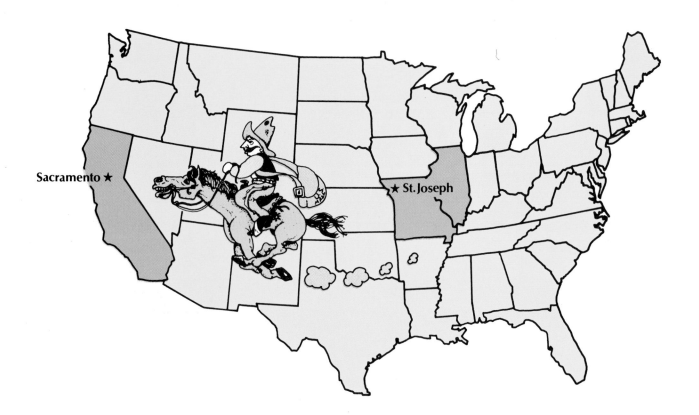

Sacramento ★   ★ St. Joseph

Lambs and Ewe

What a lovely, cozy thing a wool sweater is on a chilly evening. Don't you agree? The next time you snuggle into one, give thanks to the lamb who grew it for you.

Sheep and lambs produce a wool coat that is shaved off once a year. This is called *shearing*. Only female sheep, called *ewes*, are shorn. On a sheep ranch, the shearing can last a whole week if the herd is large. One person can shear up to a hundred ewes a day.

The next step to your sweater, scarf, or blanket is the bundling of the raw wool in bags. The bags, which often weigh two hundred or three hundred pounds, are sent to a mill where the wool is sorted by color, fineness and waviness. Very white wool, for example, is more valuable because it can be colored more easily.

All the wool is then scrubbed clean and untangled. It is spun into yarn next and sent to mills for knitting or weaving into fabrics.

The finished fabrics are sent to manufacturers who turn out the sweaters, scarves and blankets we're so happy to have when snow falls and the wind blows.

Behind the Scenes

Dairy Delights

Chocolate milk comes from chocolate cows? Wrong. Ice cream is born in scoops? Wrong. Butter begins yellow? Wrong again. All these things are made from milk. They all begin on a dairy farm where cows are milked twice a day.

There are dairy farms in every U.S. state. Wisconsin leads the country in dairy production with 10 billion quarts a year (that's 10,000,000,000). Every American eats an average of 550 pounds of dairy foods per year. You can see how important the dairy industry is to us.

Half of the milk on a dairy farm stays milk. Fresh milk is called raw milk. Raw milk, after cooling, goes through five stages. First, the cream, or fat, is separated from the milk. Then the milk is heated to kill any bad germs in it. After that, the milk is homogenized (hə-moj-ə-nighzd). This process breaks up any fat particles left in the milk to make the milk smooth. Vitamins A and D are added to the milk just before it is packaged in bottles or cartons. This is the last step before you see it in your market.

The other half of the milk produced is made into butter, cheese, ice cream and dry milk products.

Making butter is easy to do today. When farmers did it by hand, it was hard work. The farmer let raw milk stand until the cream, also called butterfat, rose to the top. He skimmed it off and put it into a *butter churn*, a closed wooden container. With a handle through the top, the cream was *churned*, which means stirring hard. It took a long time and a lot of churning to make butter.

You can try this yourself. Pour about a cup of cream into a big bowl. Beat it. First it will turn into whipped cream. Keep on beating. It will change. Part of it will look like water and part will be pale yellow lumps. Pour out the water. Spread the rest on bread. Butter!

All cheese is made from milk. It takes about 10 pounds of milk to make one pound of cheese. When milk stands for a while at room temperature, it sours. Then the tiny solid parts separate from the liquid. The liquid part is called *whey*. The solid part is called *curd*. Cheese comes from the curd.

Behind the Scenes

One look in the dairy case of your supermarket tells you there are many different kinds of cheese. But all are made in the same basic way. There are some differences in the things added to cheese to create various tastes.

Swiss cheese is unique because of the *bacteria*, a good germ, added to the curd. This bacteria forms air bubbles in the cheese. When the air bubbles burst, what remains are the famous holes in Swiss cheese.

Other cheeses, like blue cheese, use different bacteria. The bacteria in blue cheese is the same used to make penicillin, a modern wonder drug. So you see, not all germs are bad for you.

Ice cream is a simple but wonderful product made of cream, condensed milk, sugar and flavoring. The amounts of cream in ice cream vary depending on who makes it. The more cream in ice cream, the richer or creamier it is, naturally. Some ice creams have air beaten into them to make them fluffier. This kind of soft ice cream is what comes out in swirls from a machine. No matter how you eat it, though, ice cream is a true dairy delight.

Unusual Zoo

The last time you went to the zoo, you probably saw an elephant, an ostrich, and a gorilla or two. But did you see spiders, caterpillars and slugs? You didn't unless you visited the popular Insect Zoo at the San Francisco Zoo. It's one of only five insect zoos in the country.

The zoo in San Francisco holds 40 different insects and some close relatives of the insect family like crabs. Each insect has its own terrarium set up to look like the insect's natural environment. Some are tropical insects, some are desert insects and others are water insects.

The zoo has daily demonstrations. A keeper may show a tarantula and let visitors pet it as the keeper talks about this well-known spider, or the keeper may bring out the walking sticks or the Hercules beetle. All are fascinating. Did you know, for example, that all insects *molt*, or shed?

tarantula

There are also insect zoos in the Cincinnati Zoological Park, the Smithsonian Institute in Washington, D.C., the Arizona Sonora Museum of Natural History and the Portland Zoological Park in Oregon.

walking stick

caterpillar

slug

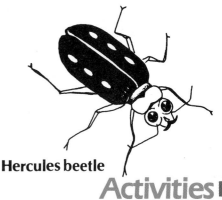

Hercules beetle

Activities ➡

Activities

Why not set up an insect zoo of your own? Catch a firefly, a caterpillar and a cricket, or any other insects in your area, each in a separate clean jar. Put a leafy branch in the jar. The jar should have holes in the lid for fresh air. Invite your friends to see the wild creatures. Talk about how they're alike and how they're different. Then let them go free the next day. In one day you can learn a lot by studying your own insect zoo.

Home Photo Zoo

You can learn a lot about animals without going to the zoo. You can even put together your own zoo. Cut pictures of animals out of magazines and paste them in a notebook or album. Write under the picture what you know about the animal. Leave room so you can add other things you learn about the animal later.

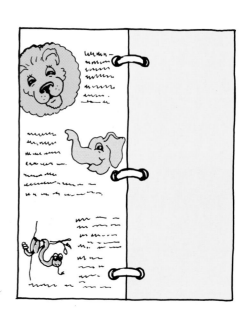

Jokes

ALICE: "What are you doing Farmer John?"
FARMER JOHN: "Feeding the Pigs."

ALICE: "Wouldn't it save time if you just shook the tree and let the apples fall to the ground?"

FARMER JOHN: "Yes, but what's time to a Pig?"

You:	Knock, knock.
Friend:	Who's there?
You:	Banana. Knock, knock.
Friend:	Who's there?
You:	Banana. Knock, knock.
Friend:	Who's there?
You:	Orange.
Friend:	Orange who?
You:	Orange you glad I didn't say banana again?

Winging It

The National Audubon Society has a special interest in wildlife. Their program for young people is called the Adventurers Club. Your school may already be involved in this program. The Club has projects that make learning about local plants and animals fun and teaches how to protect them. Go to the library to find out more about the National Audubon Society and how to get involved in the Adventurers Club.

Activities

Homemade Ice Cream

Get your parents to help, then you all can enjoy this homemade treat. Mix together two-thirds of a cup of sweetened condensed milk, one-half cup water, and one-and-a-half teaspoons of vanilla extract. Pour into freezer tray or shallow pan and freeze until little crystals form around the sides of the pan. Whip one cup of heavy cream until it forms soft peaks. Mix the whipped cream gently into the half-frozen milk and put back into the freezer. When partly frozen, scrape the mixture out, beat again until smooth, and then freeze again until the ice cream is frozen enough to eat.

A Not So Simple Chat

Did you ever notice how many times on television one person is asking another questions? About a new book? Or about the new fire house in your town? Or about anything? This question-and-answer process is called an interview. Interviews are a very important way to learn and find things out. If you would like to try it yourself, follow these easy steps:

1. Choose a *subject*. The subject is the person you want to interview. Why not start with a favorite relative?
2. Get a pad and pencil.

3. Write down your questions, leaving space in between each for the answers you will put in later. Here are some suggestions to get you started.

   - Do you have any hobbies?
   - Where did you go on your last vacation and what did you see?
   - What was your favorite subject in school when you were my age? Why?

   Now add some questions of your own.
4. Ask your subject for an *appointment*. An appointment sets the time and place you will meet to talk. Be considerate and on time for your appointment.
5. Be sure to thank your subject for the interview when it's over.

Activities

If you have a school paper, you may want to write an interview. Maybe you'd like to interview a new student. Through your interview in the paper, you can introduce the new student to everyone. Or you could interview a favorite teacher, or the school librarian.

A good idea to entertain yourself is a fantasy interview. You think of a subject to interview — Santa Claus, Superman, someone from a favorite fantasy of your own — and ask all the things you've always wanted to. On a long trip you can play the fantasy interview with your parents or a brother or sister. Miles fly by on the open highway when you're in the middle of interviewing your hero.

The interview is a very good thing to learn. Finding answers is often just a matter of asking the right questions.

Word Search

Hidden in the maze below are words you've just learned. Do you remember what they mean? The words go across and down. One word is hidden diagonally. Find the words in the maze, then write them on another paper.

EVOLUTION, SERPENTINE, WARREN, DEN, AMPHIBIAN, DOLPHIN, SYMBOL, EWE, EAGLE, INSECT

S	Y	M	B	O	L	C	E	W	E
D	E	N	J	C	L	M	A	A	V
O	N	R	O	U	X	S	G	R	O
L	B	X	P	H	C	G	L	R	L
P	P	Q	W	E	N	K	E	E	U
H	A	C	V	S	N	P	D	N	T
I	N	S	E	C	T	T	R	Z	I
N	U	V	D	H	G	W	I	A	O
C	F	I	X	M	K	J	T	N	N
A	M	P	H	I	B	I	A	N	E

Activities

Your Own Story

A journal is your own story — told by you, to yourself. Start today. Write in your journal what you did that was fun, write about people you meet, write your feelings and ideas. You don't have to write every day. When you do add something to your journal, put down the date too.

You can buy a journal or you can make one yourself. If you make one, use lined paper sheets for the inside. For the cover and back, use construction paper. Draw and color a pretty picture on the cover. Punch holes along one side of the journal (sheets, cover and back, all together). Put yarn through the holes and knot it to keep your journal together.

Family Tree

No, a family tree doesn't grow apples. It grows facts about you and your family. You can trace your *roots*, which means the beginnings, of your family, back through many years.

1. Start by putting down your father's and your mother's full names. Ask your mother if she had a different name before she married your father. It would be called her maiden name.
2. Under their names, add the dates and places of their birth, and of their marriage to one another.

3. Then add your grandparents. Add the names of your father's parents and your mother's parents to the family tree. Ask them for the same facts. Remember to use maiden names for the women.

4. Add the names of your great-grandparents (on both sides of the family) and their dates. Put down the dates, too, of any family members who are no longer alive.

5. Go back as far as you can. While you talk to your parents and grandparents about the family tree, you'll probably discover many surprising and interesting things about your past.

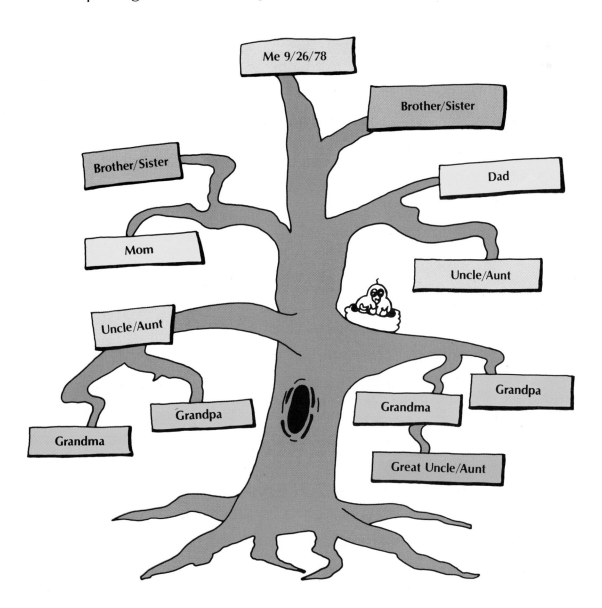

Activities

Dancing Snakes

These snakes have been dancing from morning to night. Can you get through the day without meeting one face to face? Start at MORNING and find your way through the snakes with your finger. If you get to a snake's head, back up and try another path until you reach NIGHT.

MORNING

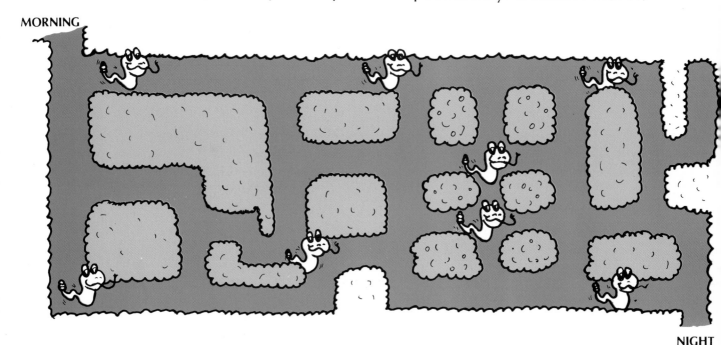

NIGHT

Animal Tag

Set up teams of players. Name them after two animals that cooperate in nature. One can be Owls. The other Prairie Dogs. (In nature, prairie dogs use burrows at night. Some burrowing owls use the same burrow during the day.) Then play animal team tag.

1. One Prairie Dog is chosen IT. The one chosen IT has to chase all the Owls.
2. When a Prairie Dog IT tags an Owl, the Owl becomes IT and has to chase all the Prairie Dogs.

3. One place—a lamp post, a fire hydrant or even a mailbox—can be named the burrow, or HOME. It's a safe spot. Anyone touching HOME cannot be tagged IT.
4. The Prairie Dogs should try to keep the Owl team members from reaching the burrow, and the Owls, when an Owl becomes IT, should try to keep Prairie Dogs from reaching the burrow.

A Woolly Spider

Here's a little woolly spider that's easy to put together. A large, empty thread spool and eight pipe cleaners are all you need.

1. Put one pipe cleaner into the middle of the spool so it shows through on the bottom.
2. Flatten the pipe cleaner end against the bottom of the spool.
3. Curve the long part of the pipe cleaner down to make one spider leg.
4. Do the same steps with the other seven pipe cleaners.
5. Now that you have a woolly spider, don't be like Miss Muffet. Let it sit down beside you.

Activities

How Much Are You Growing?

Snakes grow faster than you do. Make a snake chart to measure how much you grow from month to month. Watch yourself slowly catch up to the snake. To make the chart you'll need a roll of brown wrapping paper or 5 pieces of construction paper (8½″ x 11″), scissors, a yardstick and crayons.

1. If you start with a roll of paper, cut a piece at least 50 inches long. Or use 5 pieces of construction paper taped together tops to bottoms to make one long sheet.
2. Use a yardstick to mark inches and feet along one edge of the chart. Put a mark at 2 feet, 3 feet, 4 feet, and every inch in between. Add half-inch marks if you want, too.
3. Lay the chart flat on the floor and draw a long snake from bottom to top. Make it colorful. Give it polka dots, stripes and a big grin. Use your imagination.
4. Tape or tack your grow chart to a flat wall.
5. Stand against the chart. Draw a bow tie on your snake at the height you are now. Then, check your height whenever you feel like it to see how much you've grown.

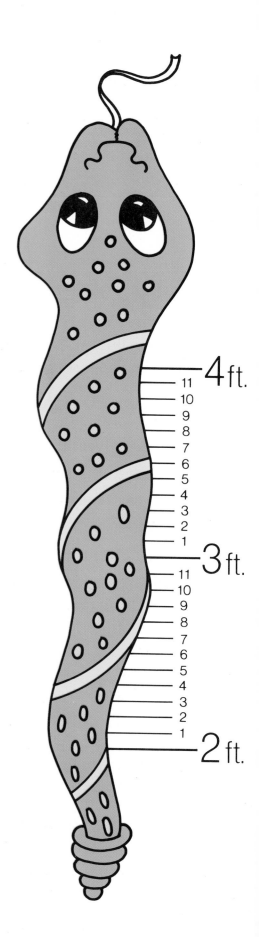

Trivia Game

Trivia are facts that may be unimportant but are very interesting. You can make up a game using trivia. Here are some to start you off. Put them on cards. Write the question on one side and the answer on the other. Stump your friends.

1. Q. Which animal has the fastest rate of growth?
    A. The blue whale. It grows from a few ounces to 100,000 pounds in one year.
2. Q. How long can the average whale stay under water without coming up for air?
    A. Two hours.
3. Q. What has a vocabulary of 32 distinct sounds but no vocal cords?
    A. A dolphin. It has a vocabulary of clicks, whistles, creaks, barks, rasps, squeals and groans.

Did You Know...?

- Certain worms spin silk thread into cocoons. Silk worms are now raised on farms. It takes 4,000 silk worms to produce only one pound of silk thread.

- Hair brushes used to be made from the bristles (or hairs) of a boar. A boar is a kind of large, wild pig.

- Down jackets are so warm because they're made from the same thing that keeps ducks and geese warm — the softest, fluffiest feathers.

Activities

Hide and Seek

Frogs can be shy. These in the picture are trying to hide from you. Look closely at the lily pads. You should find 7 frogs.

You Must Be Dreaming

In "Could Be Worse!", Grandpa has a wild dream. Choose your own dream. Just pick what you would do each time the story stops.

A. There's a big thunderstorm outside. Mom and Dad are fast asleep. You are afraid. You go to their room. You find them gone. The storm has blown open the window. Do you . . .

   • Go back to your room and hide under the covers (go to D)
   • Go to the window to close it (go to B)

B. From the window you see your parents outside talking to someone in a spacesuit who's landed a flying saucer in your yard. Do you . . .

   • Call the police and go back to your room (go to E)
   • Get a camera and photograph the spaceperson (go to C)

C. When you get to the yard, the spaceperson invites your whole family on a trip to another planet. Do you:

- Say you get sick in spaceships (go to E)
- Agree to go — in tomorrow night's dream (go to F)

D. Be braver. Dreams aren't real. They can be exciting!

E. You can have even more fun dreaming. Enjoy your imagination.

F. What a good dreamer you are! Keep it up.

Activities

"Here's Fido"

If your dog does tricks and your friends' pets do too, you have a pet show waiting to happen. Here's how to make it great.

1. First, tell your friends about the show. Set a date that's good for everyone. Allow plenty of time to practice.
2. Get a list of all the acts. Whose dog can catch a Frisbee in the air? Whose cat jumps through hoops? Does anyone have a talking bird? This list is called a program. You can write out copies to hand out to your audience at the show.
3. One week before the show, put up a notice in your neighborhood. The notice should tell where the show will be and at what time. Check with your parents first, though.
4. Make prizes. Cut small squares of light cardboard and write FIRST, SECOND and THIRD on them. You can paste blue, red and white ribbons (cut them about 2″ long) on the cardboard badge or color them in.
5. Invite a parent or a teacher to be a judge at the show.
6. Have plenty of water on hand for the animal performers. Remind your friends to bring reward treats for the pets—to reward the animals for doing their best in the show.
7. Have a great show!